This book is presented to:

_____

from:

_____

on this date:

_____

Dedication

To Micah, my creative kid with a super big heart.
I love you, son!

WHY GOD?

Big Answers
About God
and Why We
Believe in Him

DAN DEWITT
Illustrated by Christine Grove

B&H
KIDS

Nashville, Tennessee

This is Thomas and his dog, Dorothy. Thomas loves to ask questions. Silly ones and serious ones, he loves them all.

Today starts as a silly-question day. . . .

Are bats really just mice with wings? Thomas wonders. Do bats like cheese too? Can other animals grow wings?

There's Thomas's sister, Hope. She's really good at asking questions too. And that's their mom in the window. *Hi, Mom!*

Sometimes their mom helps them find answers, especially when they have a humdinger. That's a question with an extra-hard-to-find answer.

Thomas is really going to need his mom's help today.
He has a super-duper, ginormous, humdinger of a question.

"Why God?" he asks Hope. "My friend Richard at
school doesn't believe in God. So, why do we believe in Him?"

"Ooooo, that's a humdinger!" Hope says.
Dorothy just wags her tail.

Later, Thomas and Hope are helping their mom in the garden.
Dorothy helps too.

Mom had overheard their questions about God, so she asks,
"Thomas, where did our flowers come from?"

"From the seeds we planted," Thomas says.

"Where do you think the seeds came from?" she asks.

Thomas and Hope look at each other and shrug.

"From the store?" Hope says, sounding more like she
is asking a question than giving an answer.

"Well, yes, stores sell seeds. But seeds come from other flowers. When flowers grow, they make seeds for even more flowers. You can't get seeds without first having a flower," Mom explains.

Some answers make you think of even more questions, and that's what happens to Hope.

"So where did the first flower come from?" she asks.

"That's a great question," Mom says. "God made the very first flower. The Bible says that God made the whole world! He filled it with all kinds of animals like big giraffes and tiny salamanders. And He planted a garden for the first man and woman, Adam and Eve, to live in. That's how we got the first flower."

"That's a clue to point us toward God," Mom explains.

"I love clues!" Thomas says.

"Me too!" says Hope.

"Everything had to come from somewhere," Mom says.
"It couldn't just happen by accident. We can look at the
world and know Someone really powerful made it all."

"Our good God designed a just-right world. Did you know that if our planet were even a little bit closer to the sun, it would be too hot for us to live here?"

"Or if we were just a little farther from the sun, it
would be too cold for us to live here. Brrrrrrrrrr!"

"But if God made everything just right, then
what about all the bad stuff?" Hope wonders.

Thomas nods. "Like storms and floods and shark attacks." *Not everything is just right*, he thinks.

Dorothy shivers.
She doesn't like sharks either.

"Sadly, the world is broken now," Mom explains. "But our good God has promised to make the world just right again."

"Who broke the world?" Thomas asks with a giggle.

"Adam and Eve didn't obey God. That's what the Bible calls sin. Sin is why the world is no longer just right," Mom says. "And sometimes we don't obey God either, do we? But God left even more clues for us, to point us toward Him."

"Suhweet! More clues!" Thomas says.

"What are they?" Hope asks.

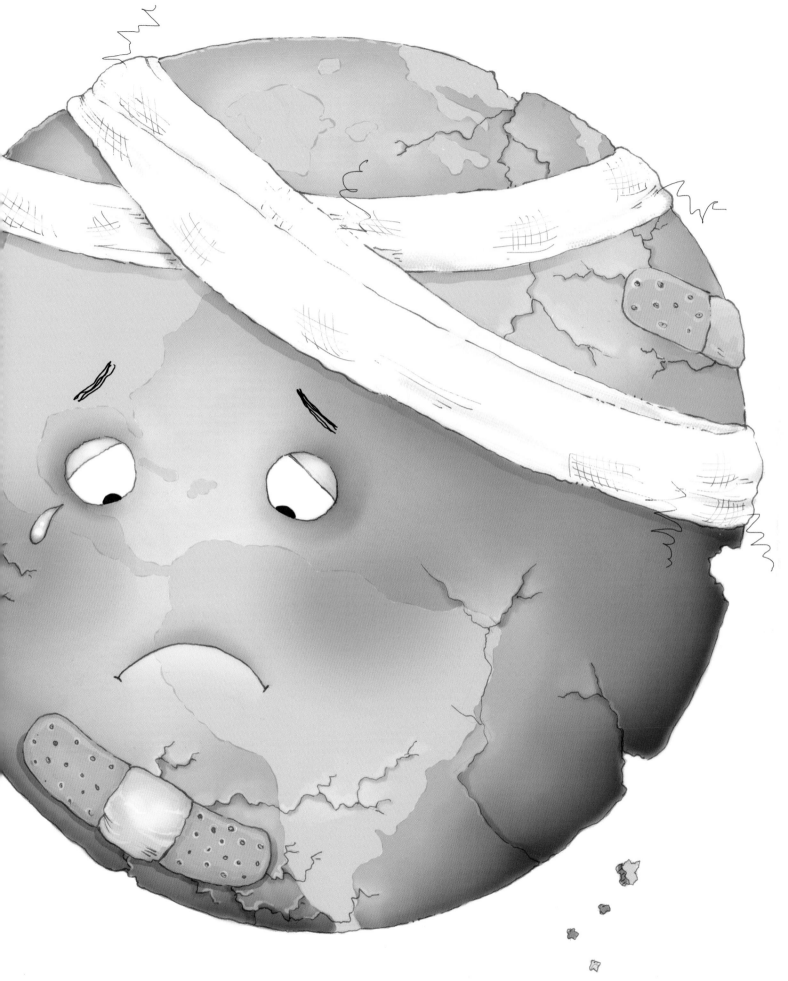

"Well," Mom says with a smile, "the Bible says God made us so that we know the difference between good and bad. That's another clue that points toward Him, because He is the Source of everything good."

"We know bad things like floods and tornados can hurt people. And we know people can do bad things and hurt each other too. We can tell that something has gone wrong with the world. Something has happened to God's *just-right* creation."

"God put these clues inside our hearts," Mom explains. "Even though the world isn't always good, God wants us to know He is real and He is good. And He wants us to do more than just know about Him, He wants us to believe in Him and trust Him too."

"Does that make sense?" she asks.

Thomas and Hope look at each other, nod, and smile.

And so does Dorothy.

God made everything

"He made this world just right so we could know His power. And He made our hearts just right so we could know His goodness," Mom says.

"So *that's* why we believe in God!" Thomas says. "Wow! We found some big answers today!"

"Yep!" Hope agrees.

"Yip!" Dorothy says.

After all these super-duper, ginormous, humdinger questions, Thomas and Dorothy are ready to sit back and start thinking silly thoughts once again.

Remember:

The heavens declare the glory of God, and the sky proclaims the work of His hands.—Psalm 19:1

Read:

Read Romans 1:18–20. Have you ever taken a drink of milk that's gone bad? Ugh! Yuk! I love milk, but when it goes sour, there is nothing worse! The Bible explains that the world is kind of like sour milk. It was once really good, but something turned it sour. That's why the apostle Paul said that we now see God's wrath—His disapproval. We can tell that what was once just right has somehow gone bad.

Still, Paul showed us that God has filled the world with clues to point us back to Him and give us reasons to believe in Him. King David said the heavens reveal the glory of God (Psalm 19). But because of our sin—our disobedience to God—we often sense God's wrath instead of thinking about how great He is. But remember, before there was sin, God made the world just right so we could know His power, and He made our hearts just right so we could know His goodness. The Bible promises that one day there will be no more sin or sadness, because God will make everything just right once again.

Think:

1. God made an amazing world, didn't He? Can you name five ways you see God's power and goodness in creation (Romans 1:20)?

2. What do you think has gone wrong with the world?

3. Because we can sense God's power and goodness in the world, Romans 1:20 says we have no excuse for not believing in Him. Do you think there are any good excuses for not believing in God?

4. Have you ever heard someone say they don't believe in God? Did they say why? If someone asked why *you* believe in God, what would be your answer?

5. So many things in the world point to God. Can you say a prayer and thank Him for these clues from creation?